"The great thing about youth sports is that they teach children so many different valuable life lessons. Football teaches us about teamwork, accountability, fair play, and builds character for young people who play this wonderful game.

Through his experiences playing youth football, all the way to the NFL, Johnny does an outstanding job describing how math plays a substantial role in both football and in our lives every day! He proves that when you have a proclivity for math, it makes football THAT MUCH more fun for a kid!"

–Jesse Palmer
Former NFL player, ESPN football analyst,
and special contributor to *Good Morning America*

First, I want to give all honor to my Lord and Savior, Jesus Christ. This book is dedicated to my biggest supporter and love of my life, Gia. My inspirations Jade, Joy, Justice, and Jamie, you all are the reason I strive daily to become a better husband, father, and man.

www.mascotbooks.com

Grant's Sports Adventures: Math & Football

©2016 Johnny Rutledge. All Rights Reserved. No part of this publication may be reproduced, stored in a retrieval system or transmitted in any form by any means electronic, mechanical, or photocopying, recording or otherwise without the permission of the author.

For more information, please contact:
Mascot Books
560 Herndon Parkway #120
Herndon, VA 20170
info@mascotbooks.com

Library of Congress Control Number: 2016907116

CPSIA Code: PRT0916A
ISBN: 978-1-63177-784-4

Printed in the United States

One sunny fall evening, Grant and his dad sat watching their favorite football team play.

"One day I'm going to play football just like those guys on T.V.," said Grant, pointing out his favorite player.

"Son, you can be anything you want to be when you grow up," his father smiled.

"But before you can win on the football field,
you must first be a champion in the classroom."

Baffled, Grant asked, "What do you mean,
a champion in the classroom?"

"You won't be able to play football forever," answered his
father, "so it's important you get an education."

"But what does school have to do with me playing football?" asked Grant.

"Everything, son! Here, let me show you."

"Football is a game of numbers so you have to
be able to understand lots of math concepts.
They're everywhere in football!"

"For example, our quarterback threw for 3,000 yards in twelve games last year. How many yards did he average passing per game?" Grant's father asked.

Grant thought hard before saying, "250 yards passing per game!"
"Right you are, son!" said Grant's father.

"My math teacher always said math could be found in everything we do. Now I think I might know what she's talking about!" said Grant excitedly.

"We're learning about angles now. Are there angles in football?"

"Remember at practice when you lined up at wide
receiver and coach showed you how to run routes?"
asked his father.

"Yes, that was fun," Grant smiled, thinking back
to practice.

"Coach taught us how to run a post, which he called an 8,
and a dig, he called that a 6, and a slant.
I think that one was a 2.

But what does that have to do with angles, Dad?"

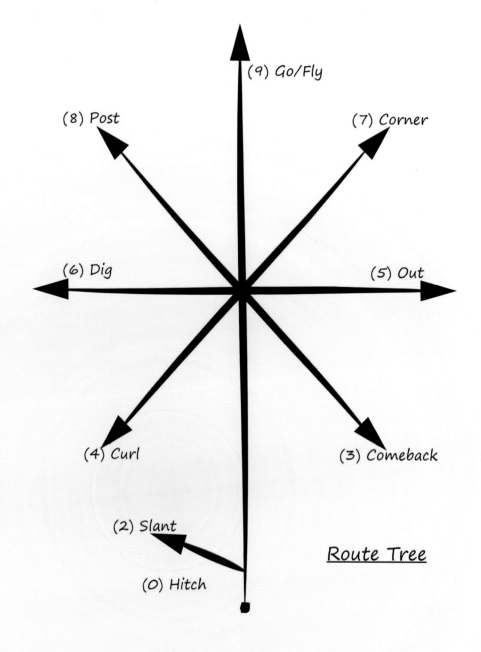

(9) Go/Fly

(8) Post   (7) Corner

(6) Dig   (5) Out

(4) Curl   (3) Comeback

(2) Slant

(0) Hitch

<u>Route Tree</u>

Grant's father replied, "What he taught you were three different routes from the passing route tree.

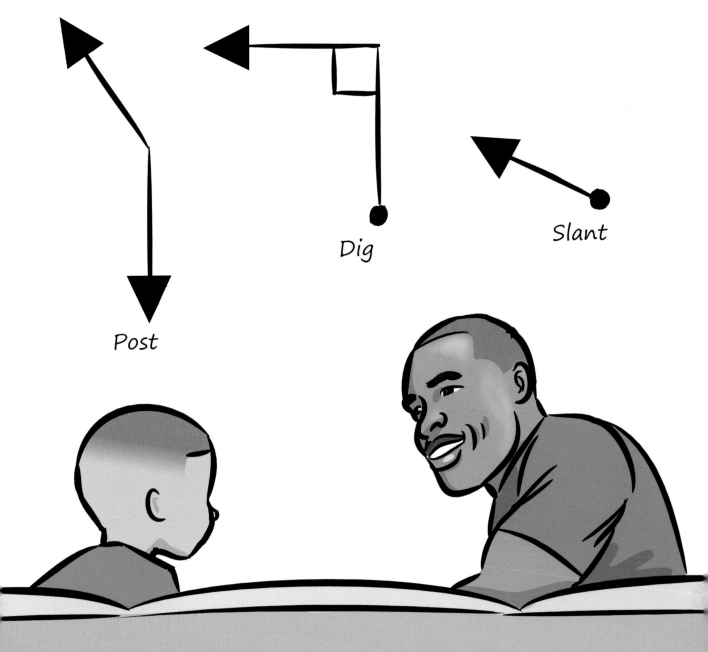

Post

Dig

Slant

The post, dig, and slant are all run at different angles."

"The post, or 8, makes an obtuse angle.

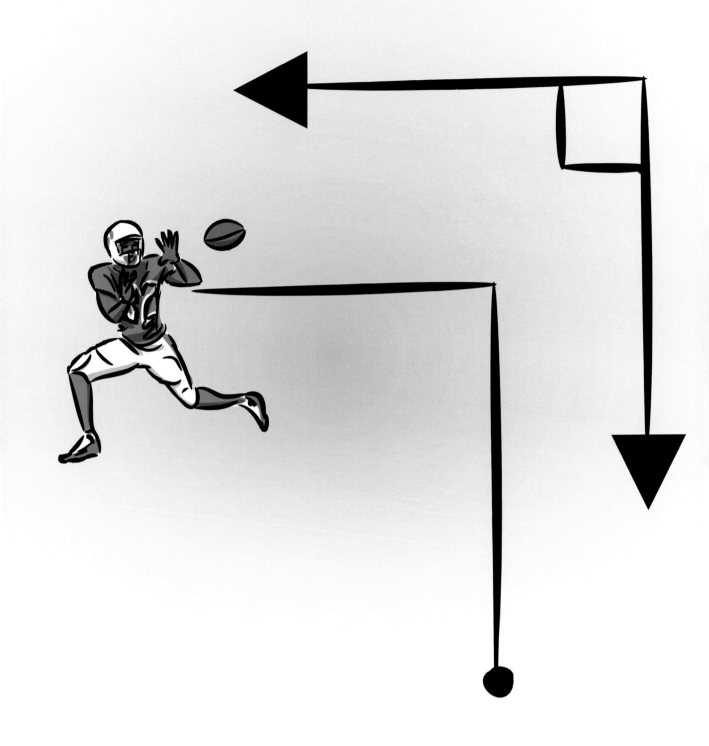

The dig, or 6, is a perfect right angle, also known as a 90 degree angle."

"And the slant, or 2, is run at an acute 45 degree angle.

The numbers 8, 6, and 2 tell you what type of route to run."

Grant's eyes grew wide as he traced the angles in the air with his finger.

Excitement bubbling up inside him, he cried, "I get it now!
Math and football!"

"My teacher was right! Math can be found in everything we do!" Grant said jumping off the couch to do his favorite victory dance.

"That's right!" said Grant's father.

"Can we have a snack at halftime?" Grant asked. "All this football, math, and dancing is making me hungry!"

30

THE END

ABOUT THE AUTHOR

Johnny Rutledge is a six-year NFL veteran, ALL-SEC linebacker at the University of Florida, scholar, coach, and youth mentor. During his playing days and in retirement, Rutledge has made it his mission to support early childhood literacy while using athletics to encourage athletes to take pride in being extraordinary students and exceptional people of character.